For Tom Vonah, good friend, and Blondie, best beach buddy ever.
– D.M

For Beau-Beau
– H.M.

First Edition 2011
Kane Miller, A Division of EDC Publishing

Text copyright © Sheryl Dianne Moritz, 2010
Illustrations copyright © Holly McGee, 2010

For information contact:
Kane Miller, A Division of EDC Publishing
PO Box 470663
Tulsa, OK 74147-0663
www.kanemiller.com
www.edcpub.com

Library of Congress Control Number: 2010927396

Manufactured by Regent Publishing Services, Hong Kong
Printed November 2010 in ShenZhen, Guangdong, China

1 2 3 4 5 6 7 8 9 10

ISBN: 978-1-935279-81-5

HUSH, LITTLE BEACHCOMBER

Written by Dianne Moritz • Illustrated by Holly McGee

Kane Miller
A DIVISION OF EDC PUBLISHING

Hey, little beachcomber, what do you say?
Let's take a trip to the beach today!

And since that beach is way too far,
let's drive there in our old red car.
So...grab a towel and your bathing suit.
Let's hit the road. Come on, let's scoot!

Look, little beachcomber, there's the pier.

How 'bout a snack and a cold root beer?

Hush, little beachcomber, don't say a word,

let's sit and watch that small shore bird.

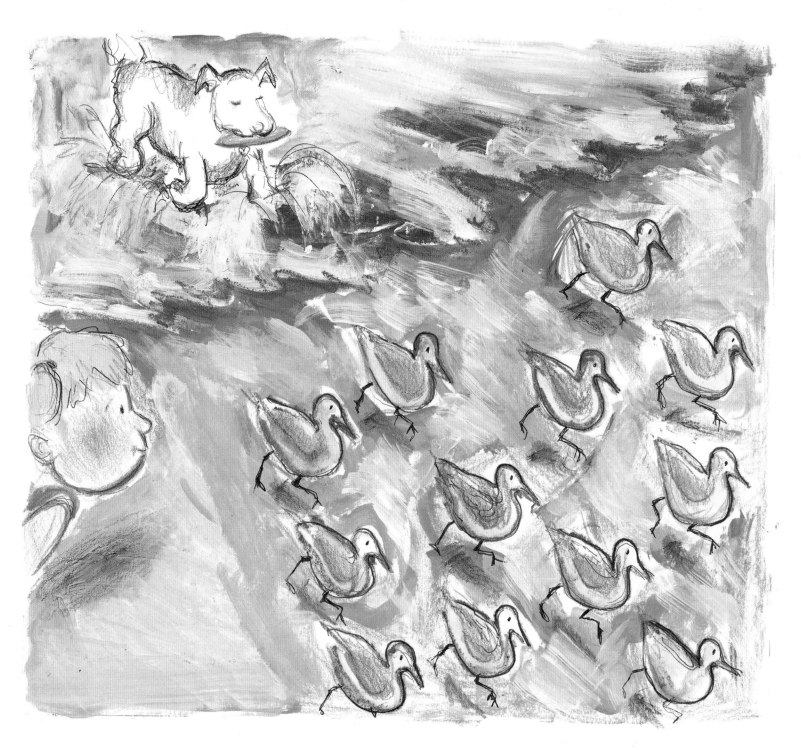

And if that shore bird runs away,

let's wade out in the cool sea spray.

And if that sea spray stings our eyes,

let's make a bunch of beach-sand pies.

And if those sand pies turn to goop,

let's stir a batch of seaweed soup.
And if that seaweed really smells,

let's go collect a few seashells.

And if that pail is full enough,

let's unpack all our picnic stuff.

And if that picnic's too much food,

let's throw our scraps to the seagull brood.

And if those seagulls nip and snap,
let's lie down for a short sun nap.

And if that sun is just too hot,

a nice, quick dip will hit the spot.

And if the surf is rough and mean,

Momma's gonna crown you Mermaid Queen.

And if those waves toss us about,

let's swim in so we don't wipeout!

And if a huge wave knocks us down,

you'll still be the best beachcomber in town!

Hush, little beachcomber, time to go home.
But first let's stop...for an ice cream cone!
Hey, little beachcomber, what do you say?

Let's come here next Saturday! Hooray!